8[00]

MW01710358

Collateral Damage

COLLATERAL DAMAGE

The Tragedy of Medea

Jackie Crossland

PRESS GANG PUBLISHERS
VANCOUVER

The Publisher gratefully acknowledges financial assistance from the Canada Council.

CANADIAN CATALOGUING IN PUBLICATION DATA

Crossland, Jackie
Collateral damage

ISBN 0-88974-042-9

A play.
I. Title.
PS8555.R612C6 1992 C812'.54 C92-091583-3
PR9199.3.C76C6 1992

First Printing September 1992
1 2 3 4 5 96 95 94 93 92

Edited by Barbara Kuhne
Cover and text design by Val Speidel
Cover illustration by Debra Rooney
Author and all character photographs by Dorothy Elias, except photograph on p. 37 by Margaret Knight
Typeset in Stempel Schneidler
Printed on acid-free paper by Best Gagné Book Manufacturers Inc.
Printed and bound in Canada

Press Gang Publishers
603 Powell Street
Vancouver, B.C. V6A 1H2
Canada

for Nora D.

CONTENTS

PLAYWRIGHT'S NOTE

A story is the sum of all its versions. There are a lot of versions of the Medea story and this is mine. When I wrote the script, I always intended for it to be played entirely by women, including the roles of men. This is a woman's story, with men presented as a woman sees them. I also intended for each actor (with two exceptions) to have at least two parts—one as a member of the CHORUS and at least one other role. In the original production, we worked with six actors playing a total of fifteen parts, including the role of Medea's mother, who is a ghost. We used a large puppet figure for MOTHER, who was visibly present throughout the play, sitting among the musicians, who were also on stage throughout. CLEO, who is the narrator of the story and the CHORUS leader, provides a consistent frame of reference. Each character presents a different facet of the story according to her particular understanding; the result is a multi-focus work which, we hope, will encourage people to consider even more versions of the story. I believe that this could be any woman's story—which is not an original notion in itself, but one that is harder and harder to hold onto in the present-day world. The many versions of a story take time to consider, and, as Medea herself says, "Time is what we never have."

Why did I call this story *Collateral Damage: The Tragedy of Medea*? "Collateral Damage" was a term used during the 1991 Persian Gulf War to describe the many thousands of civilian deaths that resulted from the bombing of Iraq. For the most part, women, children, and old people were killed, and, for the most part, the killing was shrugged off as an unavoidable consequence of the political and economic struggles over which those who died had no control. Similarly, the women and children in this play are buffeted by circumstances over which they have no control. The tragic part of the story stems from this: a mother, Medea, is separated from her children by such circumstances and never gets to see them grow up.

Why is this play set in an East Vancouver kitchen, filled with utensils and toys that might be found in any house with children? Because, like many women, I do a great deal of my thinking and talking and sorting through of the many versions of stories that make up my life while I am surrounded by the mundane. I regard this as an important element in the whole, not as a dreary fact of existence. In the production of this play we also used music, masks and puppets, approaching it as a theatrical comedy. This may appear at odds with its title, but we all felt very much at home with this approach. I wrote this play not to glorify the heroes, the villains, or their victims, but to encourage myself and other women to appreciate our value, and to encourage us to rise.

PRODUCTION NOTES

Cast of Characters

Cleo
Chorus (Cleo's Friends/Family): Annie, Brenda, Sonia, Zelda
Medea
Maid
Princess
Jason
Sailor
Mother (Ghost)
Brother
Father
Messenger
Crayon
Temple Woman
Queen

Collateral Damage: The Tragedy of Medea was first performed at the Vancouver International Fringe Festival in September 1991, co-produced by Random Acts Productions and Concerted Effort Productions. It was directed by Jackie Crossland, with music direction by Jacqui Parker-Snedker and original music by Jacqui Parker-Snedker and Sue McGowan. The cast were Murlane Carew, Shaira Holman, Jane Kalmakoff, River Light, Sue McGowan, and Nora D. Randall. Musicians were Martina Griffiths, Jacqui Parker-Snedker, Patti Powell, and Carol Weaver. Set, mask, prop and puppet design was by Christina Farmilo and costumes by Kate Nelson. The stage manager was Kim Barsanti, the publicist was Ann McDonell, and production assistants were Doug Butt, Malcolm Inglis, and Laura Mervyn. Poster design by Debra Rooney. Video by Carla Wolf. Photography by Margaret Knight and Christina Farmilo.

It was subsequently performed at the Vancouver East Cultural Centre in December 1991, co-produced by Random Acts Productions and Concerted Effort Productions, directed by Jackie Crossland, with music direction by Jacqui Parker-Snedker and original music by Jacqui Parker-Snedker and Sue McGowan. The cast were Murlane Carew,

Shaira Holman, Jane Kalmakoff, River Light, Sue McGowan, and Nora D. Randall, with musicians Andrea Kohl, Jacqui Parker-Snedker, Patti Powell, and Carol Weaver. Set, mask, prop and puppet design was by Christina Farmilo and costumes by Kate Nelson. Lighting design was by Ann Ravin; poster design by Debra Rooney; video by Carla Wolf. The stage manager was Kim Barsanti and the publicist was Ann McDonell. Production assistants were Jean Caha and Laura Mervyn.

For the Vancouver East Cultural Centre production an original song, *Tight Chains and Tears,* was produced on audio tape. It was written by Jacqui Parker-Snedker and Sue McGowan and performed by them with Jane Kalmakoff, Patti Powell, and Carol Weaver. Audio engineering by Jean Caha, with assistance from Jewel Neave.

Setting

The play is set in CLEO's household. The stage areas we used represented the kitchen, the adjoining deck, and the back yard. We used tape lines to separate the areas, but riser levels could also be used. In the kitchen area there were chairs, a table, and a kitchen cabinet. The deck area had a laundry tree and basket, as well as a short stepladder and small "rebounder" trampoline. The stepladder was used as MEDEA's temple wall and the trampoline served as CRAYON's throne. The yard had a child's wading pool and an over-size rocking-horse. The CHORUS characters occupy the kitchen when not playing other characters. In acting out MEDEA's story, the actors used only the deck and yard areas. Masks were stored in the kitchen cupboard, which was upstage, to simplify transformation from CHORUS to masked character. Costume and prop pieces were stored there, too, as well as on the laundry tree, in the laundry basket, and in the wading pool, as needed. An inflatable globe of the world was suspended above the stage over the deck area, and could be raised and lowered as needed. This household setting encompasses the whole story. The actors arrange props and set pieces as required for its telling.

The Characters

As mentioned in the Playwright's Note, we used six actors to play a total of fifteen roles. This is an ensemble piece with a great deal of simultaneous and overlapping action and it is important for the working out of the story that all performers be on stage at all times. There is some latitude about the division of roles; they may be changed around to suit a particular production's needs if the following requirements are kept in mind:

The role of CLEO provides a central focus for the piece. The actor in this role should not have additional roles unless necessary (in the first production, the actor playing this part also did the BROTHER—a two-line part).

MOTHER is a ghost. She comes from a "different world," but her constant presence on stage adds a great deal to the piece. In the first production, she was a large puppet, over 10 feet tall. Her words were often enhanced by music and singers, and, when not actively involved in a scene, she sat upstage with the musicians, always visible. There may be other ways of getting the same effect.

In the first production, MEDEA, JASON, CRAYON, PRINCESS and MAID were played by masked actors who also played CHORUS and other parts in the following combinations: MEDEA/ANNIE; ZELDA/ JASON/QUEEN; CRAYON/MAID/BRENDA; PRINCESS/SAILOR/ MESSENGER/TEMPLE WOMAN/SONIA. Medea's FATHER was never seen on stage. His lines were spoken by the whole cast in unison. Other combinations may be possible, but the idea of CHORUS characters transforming into other roles is important.

Music

Musicians and singers were on stage throughout the play, providing a soundscape/matrix for the piece.

Collateral Damage

ACT 1 · SCENE 1

SINGERS START THE "LAND OF DREAMS" ROUND.

Singers: In the land of dreams, giants live
in the dreams of giants, women live
like giants in the land of dreams.

AS THEY SING, MEDEA'S MOTHER LEADS THE ACTORS IN AND TAKES HER PLACE. ACTORS ENTER CARRYING GROCERY BAGS FULL OF SHOPPING AND START PUTTING ITEMS AWAY.

Chorus/Brenda: I see you've got a full house again.

Cleo: Hides the dirt.

Chorus/Sonia: Look at all this stuff.

Chorus/Annie: I have something to tell you.

Cleo: What is it, honey?

Chorus/Zelda: What is it, honey?

Chorus/Sonia: That was a good deal.

Chorus/Zelda: I didn't know this was still on the market.

Cleo: You have to keep an eye out for it.

Chorus/Sonia: (HOLDING UP THE FLEECE.) What should I do with this?

Chorus/Zelda: What is it, anyway?

Cleo: The Golden Fleece. Here, I'll get it out of your way. (SHE HANGS IT UP ON THE CLOTHESLINE.)

Chorus/Sonia: You want a coffee?

Chorus/Annie: Sure.

Chorus/Sonia: What are you up to, anyway?

Chorus/Annie: He wants me to go with him.

Chorus/Zelda: Go where?

Chorus/Annie: You don't have a chair. Here's one. Have a seat.

Chorus/Zelda: Now isn't that just like you? Always thinking about others. I feel just like I'm at home.

Cleo: Don't get too comfortable, you bunch. This is my home and don't you forget it.

Chorus/Sonia: We won't.

Chorus/Zelda: So long as we can always come back.

Chorus/Sonia: For a while.

Chorus/Zelda: For a rest.

Chorus/Sonia: For comfort.

Chorus/Zelda: Home.

Cleo: What a bunch.

Chorus/Sonia: What about that coffee?

Cleo: Help yourself to whatever there is.

Chorus/Zelda: Thanks.

Chorus/Sonia: When are you leaving?

Chorus/Annie: Two weeks.

Cleo: Have you told your mother?

Chorus/Annie: Not yet.

Chorus/Zelda: A little surprise for mumsie?

Chorus/Sonia: Have a cookie.

Cleo: If it's not one thing it's another.

Chorus/Zelda: Another what? What's going on around here, anyway?

Chorus/Sonia: I wonder if I could stay for a few days.

Cleo: Sure.

Chorus/Sonia: Just till I get on my feet.

Chorus/Zelda: This place is just open house. I've never seen the like.

Cleo: It's true. What can I say?

Chorus/Brenda: She shouldn't go back if she doesn't want to.

Chorus/Sonia: And you shouldn't leave, if you don't have to.

Chorus/Annie: He says he loves me.

Chorus/Zelda: Who loves you, honey?

Chorus/Sonia: Leave her alone.

Chorus/Annie: They treat me like a baby. I just feel so hemmed in. What should I do?

Chorus/Sonia: What you have to, I guess.

Chorus/Annie: And he does love me.

Cleo: Love . . . that's what it looks like now . . . (LAYING OUT A GAME OF SOLITAIRE.) Blazing headlines in the checkout line at the Supersave this morning—"Hero Caught in Royal Love Nest: Wife Goes Nuts and Kills Kids—Shocked Palace Staff Refuse to Comment on Disappearance of Princess." Hot stuff, eh? Happens all the time. It will probably get on the TV movie-of-the-week next week. I'm picking through the frozen peas. My neighbour says, "How could she do such a thing? Maybe she was on drugs." "No, that's not it," I says. "I don't like to brag, but it's no news to me what people get up to." It's an old story. I didn't even buy a copy of the paper.

Chorus/Sonia: What would be the point? It's an old story.

CLEO CONTINUES TO PLAY SOLITAIRE. MEDEA BEGINS TO PACE THE TEMPLE WALL AND THE STORY BEGINS TO UNFOLD AS CLEO TELLS IT.

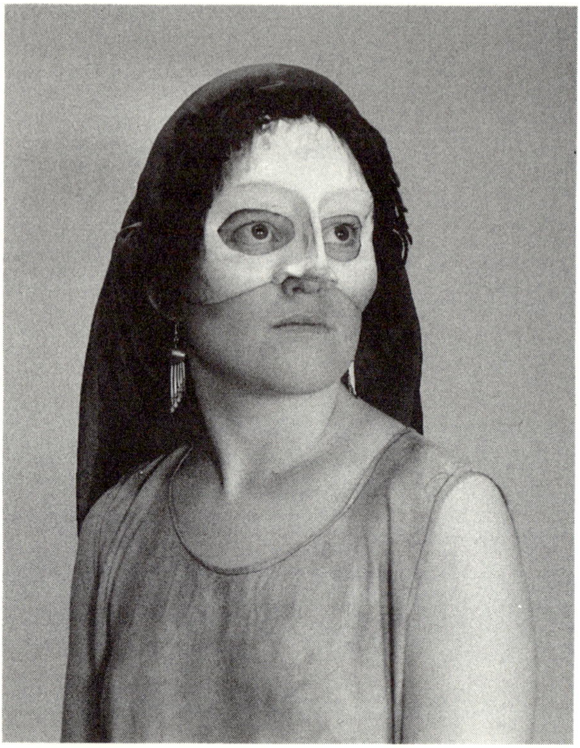

MEDEA. Watching.

Chorus/Zelda: It's a hot summer day a long time ago in Colchis. Medea is watching the Golden Fleece. She walks around the temple wall, never losing sight of the Fleece. Her maid watches at a distance.

Cleo: So, Medea is a princess. Her father has her in the temple watching the Golden Fleece. This Golden Fleece has been taken off a golden flying ram and it is very famous. Many people think it is an important thing, because gold. It is not actually used for anything. It just sits there, and like anything else with no function, it causes more trouble than it's worth.

When the story starts, Medea is doing her princess thing; the Golden Fleece is in the temple.

The other woman is the maid. All these princess types have maids. She watches Medea watch the Fleece, from a distance. Sometimes she gets bored because it's hot and she has nothing to do except hang around until they find a use for her, so maybe we'll let her take a little nap because the princess isn't looking anyhow.

THE MAID TAKES A NAP.

Chorus/Sonia: In another country called Corinth, another princess paces the palace walls and sometimes stops to look out to sea.

Chorus/Zelda: Is she waiting for love?

Chorus/Sonia: I don't think so. I hope she is looking for opportunities.

Cleo: Actually, I don't know much about princesses. But I do know about maids, because I have what you might call experience in the field. When I left school, that was one of the two jobs I could get. The other was waitress.

Of course in real life I was never the maid of a princess. Actually, I was only ever called "maid" in a couple of jobs. I was usually referred to as "the help" or "the girl." I mostly worked for families where both parents worked outside the home and there were no spare grandparents. Once or twice, I had fancier set-ups: a doctor's wife, a businessman's wife . . . One thing I remember in these fancier jobs is the time passing so slowly while I waited for them to remember I was there and to give me another chore to do. I would finish the laundry, or the floors, or diaper the baby . . . and wait . . . to be told what to do, or wait to be called for an errand. The trick would be to remain within earshot to hear them call, but far enough away so they didn't think I was prying into their business, or so they wouldn't remember me too easily and give me a chore, like ironing, which I hated, or they wouldn't get mad because I never volunteered.

So there is the maid, a bit in the distance, but not too far away.

Medea, the princess, is watching the Fleece. She strolls around the temple walls and looks out over the countryside. She watches for robbers. The temple is built on a hill and has high protective walls so it's quite safe. Medea, strolling . . .

Chorus/Sonia: And so is that other princess . . .

Cleo: The sun is shining.

Watching the Golden Fleece is not the only thing Medea does. She is called a witch and has been credited with both medical and agricultural developments. Between you and me, there are a lot of grisly stories about her but all we know for sure is that she has a great garden. In the market, where people get together, like we do at the Supersave except maybe they aren't in such a hurry all the time like we are here—of course I'm just guessing about that—anyway, at the market there is gossip. Someone, her father or her brother, would like to get rid of her at some point, and they have started these nasty rumours to justify some ugly accident later on.

You know how things are in families—all those secrets. Royal families are no different.

SINGERS START THE "MOON RISE" ROUND.

Singers: The Moon Rises
the Sun Sets
the Moon Sets
the Sun Rises.

Chorus/Sonia: The other princess goes to look for her horse.

Chorus/Zelda: Medea and the maid get out paint and brushes and start to paint one of the temple walls.

Cleo: One day, Medea is in the temple. Painting a wall. The maid helps. They do not talk. Paint. Paint . . .

DRUNKEN SAILORS APPROACH, MAKING NOISE.

Medea: What's that noise?

THE MAID LOOKS OUT OVER THE WALL.

Maid: A bunch of men are staggering up the hill. They are sailors from Greece, I think, who came to Colchis on a ship called the Argos.

THE ARGOS APPEARS.

Medea: Oh.

Maid: The Argos is in port for a week or so, laying in supplies.

Medea: Mmmm.

JASON MOVES AWAY FROM THE GROUP OF SAILORS.

Maid: That one is Jason, captain of the Argos, and I guess those others must be his shipmates.

Sailor: (GESTURING.) That is Colchis and that is our boat.

Maid: It looks like they've been drinking quite a lot in the tavern, and now they are out on the prowl . . . I wonder if they've heard about the Golden Fleece.

JASON BANGS ON THE TEMPLE WALL.

Jason: Maybe they keep it in here.

Maid: Question answered.

Jason: I've heard about it . . .

Medea: Who hasn't?

Jason: . . . but I've never seen it.

Medea: Close the gates.

Maid: Slam.

Medea: Slam.

Cleo: Slam.

THE MAID PUTS AWAY THE PAINT AND BRUSHES AND LIGHTS A LANTERN. SHE TAKES THE LANTERN TO MEDEA. MEDEA WATCHES THE SAILORS AND JASON TRY TO OPEN THE TEMPLE GATES; THEN THEY GRADUALLY GIVE UP AND FALL ASLEEP, SNORING.

Medea: What do you think?

Maid: I don't think much of them at all. A bunch of drunks.

Medea: I kind of like their captain.

Maid: He does snore louder than the rest.

Medea: If he were not drunk, I would like to sleep with him.

Maid: Oh.

Medea: You have no romance in you. That's your trouble.

Maid: It's no trouble to me.

Medea: Think how far they've come. Don't you ever want to see more of the world?

Maid: That's a very different thing.

Medea: I need an adventure. It's harder and harder to live at home.

Maid: Why?

Medea: I think my father and brother are out to get me.

Maid: Why do you think that?

Medea: I really cannot tell.

Maid: Will not tell. You know but you will not tell.

Medea: What does it matter to you?

Maid: If you don't tell, nothing can change.

Medea: What can change if I tell you? Even if you believe me, what good would that do?

Maid: I don't know. I cannot tell.

JASON WAKES UP.

Jason: I must have slept. It was ugly. What is this godforsaken place? I want to go home, wherever that is. Hey, buddy, buddy . . . no answer . . . everybody sleeping . . . hey give us a drink. It's not too much to ask. I'm not a complicated person. I'm a sailor and a fighter. I prefer the sailing to the fighting, but I don't mind a good scrap now and then.

Cleo: He likes women to be silent and soft, like a lot of guys. He has never actually met any women like that, but he is hoping to.

Jason: I go from war to war. There are lots to choose from.

Cleo: One of my personal things is to keep track of the wars. I mark them on this globe with little red dots that you buy in packages in stationery stores. Hot spots we call them nowadays. Why red? Red is for hot. Red is for blood.

One thing about wars is that rape and pillage are always part of the picture. Any war you read about or see on the TV, they will always have a story where the enemy side raped women of the other side. This story is always told to show how the enemy side is just a bunch of animals. And also, I think, to scare women so they don't step out of line while the men are away. As for Jason, he sometimes rapes in a routine kind of way, because he worries about what people think of him, particularly his sailors, and it is important to seem like a regular guy. He doesn't like this much, but it's part of the job. If

CLEO. Some things about war.

the terrified woman fights back, she sometimes can get away from him.

Jason: I've seen a lot of terrified women. It makes me tired. I don't like my job much, like a lot of people, but I do it because what would happen if everybody stopped doing their job?

Cleo: What would happen if everyone stopped doing their job?

Singers: In the land of dreams, giants live
in the dreams of giants, women live
like giants in the land of dreams.

Jason: Even after I wake up, I'm tired. I'd rather sail than fight, rather fight than fuck, rather fuck than drink, rather drink than sleep, because my dreams hurt me.

Medea: (FROM THE TEMPLE WALL.) Dreaming is good for you. You should dream, even though the stories of your dreams frighten you.

Jason: And waking is no better. My memories scare me.

Medea: All we dream and all we remember is the meaning of our life, and the dreams and the memories come when they wish and not when we call them, and all the life of our days are spent in filling other people's wishes.

Jason: How do you know all this stuff?

Medea: I have been taught to comfort people.

Jason: Are you alone?

Medea: I have a brother and a father, both, and my mother is dead.

Jason: This woman sure knows a lot. An educated woman. And her voice is not too loud. Maybe she's what I need.

Medea: It is time for me to pick one out for myself. This is risky but he is good-looking and he is leaving town soon, so maybe the rest can take care of itself.

Maid: I hope you know what you're doing.

Medea: Let him in.

THEY OPEN THE TEMPLE DOOR AND JASON ENTERS.

Medea: Help him bathe, poor thing.

Maid: He stinks of wars and rapes and ships and truly frightful wine.

Medea: I am hoping to change all that.

Maid: What are you up to, anyway?

Medea: I have to take my life into my own hands.

Maid: Be careful.

Medea: That's just the point. If I am careful, nothing will change. Talk is not enough. I must do something.

CLEO AND THE MAID BATHE JASON AND DRY HIM. THEN MEDEA AND JASON LIE DOWN TOGETHER AND MAKE LOVE.

Chorus/Brenda: I suppose there is no point in telling her to stay away from him.

Cleo: I don't suppose it would do any good.

Chorus/Brenda: The young never listen.

Cleo: You have to let them make up their own minds.

Chorus/Brenda: This will all end in tears.

Cleo: Maybe . . . we'll see. In the morning, while the maid is serving them bread and honey and almonds and some kind of goat cheese—I forgot to say there are goats—the rest of the sailors wake up, clueless. They find a stream and wash in it. They find that all the wine is gone and they need a drink something awful.

Sailor: I need a drink something awful.

Cleo: They drift back to the market, only wondering a little bit what happened to Jason.

All: Days pass.

Maid: I try to stay out of the way, appearing only to serve food, to draw bath water, to light lanterns when I am called. And a job is a job. Maybe I'll finish painting the wall.

Chorus/Sonia: Maybe she'll finish painting the wall.

Jason: Okay. Let me see it.

Medea: No.

Jason: Please, pretty please.

Medea: I can't.

Jason: Just once. Just a little peek?

Medea: All right, come on. It's no big deal, really. It just hangs there.

Jason: The Golden Fleece.

Medea: The Golden Fleece.

Maid: I wouldn't mind if she knew what she was doing, but she just caves in to his every wish.

Jason: I like it. How does it look? Can I have it?

Medea: Actually, it belongs to my brother.

Jason: What does he use it for?

Medea: He doesn't. It has no use. But my father and brother put me in the temple to guard it.

Jason: Do they come here often?

Medea: Not often.

Jason: I have an idea.

Medea: You have?

Jason: We could take it and leave this place.

Medea: And then what?

Jason: We could go someplace else.

Medea: Where would we go?

Jason: Corinth. It's much bigger than this place, much more important.

Medea: What would we live on?

Jason: We could sell this.

Medea: I don't know.

Jason: We could get quite a bit for it and live well until we get settled.

Medea: Settled?

Jason: Yes. You and me and maybe a baby or something.

Medea: A baby?

Jason: What do you think?

Medea: I don't know.

Jason: What is your name again?

Medea: Medea.

Jason: Medea, that's a nice name. A very nice name.

Medea: Thank you.

Jason: And you are very beautiful, and you do not laugh at me, even though I believe my penis is smaller than average size.

Medea: Oh, I've seen small and I've seen big and, one way or another, it doesn't make any difference to me.

Maid: It is time to prepare yet another meal of bread and cheese and honey. Maybe this time I'll throw in a handful of olives.

Medea: Give me some time.

Jason: I don't have all day.

Medea: I'll think about it.

Cleo: Now there's a lot of reasons that women hook up with men, but when you're young I think getting away from home is the biggest one.

Chorus/Brenda: It was for me.

Cleo: Well, there you go.

Chorus/Brenda: Her poor mother. It will break her heart.

Cleo: You can't stop them. They have to learn.

Chorus/Sonia: Her mother is no help to her.

Cleo: She could be . . .

Chorus/Sonia: Here's hoping.

JASON. A woman can't expect much.

Medea: I would like to get the hell out of the temple and Colchis . . . but is this the only way? (THE MAID BRINGS THE MEAL.) Leave me alone, I'm thinking. (THE MAID LEAVES.) This Jason is not a clever man. But he is brave in the way that men are and handsome. Of course, I've said that before. He pays more attention to his muscles than my conversation, which he does not seem to understand most of the time. But they say love is often like that and that a woman can't expect much.

Cleo: At last, Medea sees the ghost of her mother.

MEDEA'S MOTHER MOVES, REACHING FOR MEDEA.

Mother: I died before I could tell you . . .

Medea: Tell me what, Mother?

Mother: . . . before I could tell you to never turn your back on your father. He'd as soon stab you as look at you. He hates women and he hated me and murdered me and he will turn his attentions to you before I am cold in my grave. Mark my words, he will try to fuck you. That goes for your brother, too. He is learning his moves from his dad.

Medea: Mother, that warning is too late.

Mother: Oh my poor baby, I'm so sorry. I couldn't help you.

Medea: Mother, never mind that now. What should I do to save myself? To make things different?

Mother: I don't know . . . I'm sorry . . . I will try to think of something.

Medea: Mother . . .

Cleo: But the ghost of her mother disappeared.

Medea: Why did she come here at all if she couldn't be of any use?

Jason: What was that?

Medea: A ghost.

Jason: Oh. It's cold.

Cleo: Medea goes to stroll alone on the temple walls and think. Jason, left on his own for a time, exercises and eats.

Jason: Where's my dinner?

Maid: I don't like the way this is going.

Chorus/Sonia: Will it help to remember her mother's death?

Chorus/Brenda: Medea remembers her mother's death.

Medea: I was alone. Then my father came. I was terrified.

Cleo: She was terrified.

Chorus/Sonia: But she wasn't stupid.

Medea: I covered myself.

Chorus & Cleo: She covered her head with desiccated field rats which her father found disgusting and he sent her away to the temple, hoping she would see reason.

Chorus/Sonia: She didn't.

Cleo, Sonia & Brenda: Sometimes he sent her brother to visit her there, and he was thin and mean. She did not fight him off, but let him rub against her. Thankfully, he never took his clothes off, as this was his father's privilege. His visits disgusted her.

Cleo: She vowed to herself that she would get out of this mess somehow.

Medea: Why couldn't Mother help me? She was dead. Stay alive at all costs. That's the lesson there.

Chorus/Brenda: The girl does have a certain amount of backbone.

Cleo: She'll need it.

Medea: All right, I've thought about it. I guess, Jason, the best thing for me to do is to go away with you.

Jason: Good.

Medea: I hope so.

Jason: Listen, it'll be great. You'll love it. We'll be happy. We really will. I'm your guy. That's a promise.

Cleo: And off he goes. Back to the ship to get ready.

Chorus/Brenda: Well, he got what he wanted.

Cleo: He's not a bad guy.

Chorus/Sonia: Suddenly you're on his side.

Cleo: He's just doing what he knows.

JASON, CLEO, and MEDEA. A chance to see a bit of the world.

Chorus/Sonia: Which isn't much.

Cleo: You don't like what she's going to do. I don't either. But she has to turn the world upside down for herself. To find her place in it. In a way, it's her own business.

Medea: (TO THE MAID.) Pack my things—and your own.

Cleo: This is how the maid learns that she will be travelling to Corinth. The news takes her by surprise at first, but when she thinks about it, it seems to make sense. What else can Medea do? As for herself, her life will not amount to much without Medea.

Maid: A servant rides on her mistress's fortune. This is something my grandmother often said.

Cleo: Though this is just a story, some parts of it are for sure true. The grandmother's saying is one of the true things. I've had a lot of jobs in my time, but the ones where I lived in were the ones where they had the most control over my life. For example, if the family moved, I could move with them, or quit. That's it for choices. So I can see why the maid didn't quit. For one, it was a chance to see a bit of the world. And for two, if she quit, what would she do next? She might get into trouble for not warning Medea's father and brother. She might end up out of a job and out on her ass or even land up in jail. Better to go along with Medea.

So the maid packed.

Chorus/Sonia: One night, when it gets dark, Jason comes for the Fleece and Medea . . .

Cleo: . . . and the maid, of course.

Chorus/Sonia: . . . and the maid, course.

Medea: And my maid, of course.

Jason: Your maid?

Medea: I am a princess. I go nowhere without my maid.

Jason: Oh, right. Women are so complicated.

Chorus/Sonia: Medea gives the Golden Fleece to Jason.

MEDEA'S BROTHER ARRIVES.

Brother: What's going on here?

Jason: Who's this?

Medea: My brother.

Brother: What's going on?

JASON RUNS HIM THROUGH WITH A SWORD.

Medea: Why did you kill him? You could have just knocked

him out.

Jason: Never mind that now. Let's get out of here.

Cleo: When her father discovers the body of his dead son, he makes up a story that goes like this:

Medea cast Jason under a spell, because she is a witch. She killed her own brother and dismembered the body and threw the pieces out of the back of a chariot to confuse pursuers. Then he said:

Father/All: The girl's off her head. Ever since her mother died, she hasn't been right.

Cleo: Although people don't necessarily believe the old man, they had seen Medea with dead rats on her head, and everyone agreed that it was scary. What nobody says is . . .

Chorus/Sonia: Even if she did kill this guy and cut him into thirty pieces—why? Murderers aren't born like that. What has been done to her to make her so full of rage that she could do such a thing? And another thing—what really happened to her mother?

Cleo: Well, this is the kind of question that isn't usually asked.

Chorus/All: We sail under cover of darkness.

Cleo: I don't know what her father is up to with his fanciful story, but I think the rest of the people in Colchis just want to get by in life without too many hard questions. It's not a pretty picture.

Jason and Medea have sailed off. With the maid. And the drunk sailors. They are well out of port by dawn.

So now everyone is on the boat.

SINGERS START THE "SEA" ROUND

All (except Cleo): The sea the wind the waves

JASON, MEDEA, and the MAID. Sailing under the cover of darkness.

the sea the wind the waves
the water heaving
the sails suffing
the sea the wind the waves.

THE BOAT SAILS. MEDEA AND THE MAID ARE IN THE CABIN WITH JASON.

Cleo: This is not altogether wonderful. For one thing, the other sailors are jealous that Jason, being captain of the ship, gets to bring a woman on board. Medea mostly stays in their cabin, at Jason's suggestion. Jason tells her it's for her own protection.

Jason: It's for your own protection.

Maid: But what about me?

Medea: What about you?

Maid: Where will I stay?

Medea: Where will my maid stay?

Jason: Oh, anywhere on the boat. She'll be fine.

Medea: You'll be fine.

Maid: The other sailors will make me common property.

Medea: Oh.

Maid: Tell him.

Medea: The other sailors will make her common property.

Jason: Oh.

Maid: There is no other safe place on this boat. Let me stay with you.

Medea: Let her stay with me.

Jason: Oh.

Maid: There won't be so much fighting on board.

Medea: There won't be so much fighting on board.

Jason: Right. That's fine with me. I don't want a lot of fighting on board.

Medea: You will stay here with me.

Maid: Thank you.

Medea: You worry too much. I will always look after you as Jason will look after me. You should be happy. We are going to this new place where things will be better. You'll see.

Maid: We'll see.

Cleo: But, in fact, the maid is safe. She finds a corner for herself. When Jason and Medea make love, she pre-

MOTHER and MEDEA. "Mother, you don't make much sense."

tends she is sleeping, or that she is absorbed in her sewing.

There is a window in the cabin. Medea looks out at the sea which is very blue. She lies on the bed and dreams.

Chorus/All: She dreams that she is larger than life, that she can tear trees up by their roots, that she can wrap her arms around the moon. Once she dreams that a virgin princess made of fire and honey opens her robe and gathers Medea in and together they fly on the princess's horse to visit Medea's mother, who is seated on a stone, drinking an infusion of berries and leaves.

Mother: Medea, I've been thinking about you. I'm so happy to see you again. Are you well?

Medea: Yes, Mother.

Mother: Personally, I hate travelling. Life on board ship is so cramped.

Medea: Yes, that's true.

Mother: Your hair is so pretty.

Medea: Mother, you didn't bring me here to talk about my hair.

Mother: I thought you wanted to come.

Medea: Why did you think that?

Mother: Didn't you?

Medea: Well, of course . . .

Mother: And now we are here.

Medea: What for?

Mother: I think it would be nice to chat. We never talked much.

Medea: No.

Mother: Well, say something now that we have the chance.

Medea: Things will be better now. Jason will look after me.

Mother: How will he do that?

Medea: With his love.

Mother: Is that enough?

Medea: I'm not sure.

Mother: Always watch your back. And no matter what they say to you, always remember the sweetest apples are at the top of the tree. Stay light enough to get up there and pluck them.

Medea: Mother, you don't make much sense.

Mother: I don't now, but I'm working on it. And later, you'll

JASON and the SAILOR. What is wrong with this picture?

see what I mean.

Medea: I hope so.

Cleo: Her mother, the virgin princess and the horse are all gone. Medea wakes up.

Medea: I don't know what to make of it all.

Cleo: The Argos sails on and on through the blue Aegean. There is good weather all the way, and no trouble. Well, not much anyway.

The cabin boy, who is a sulky, though good-looking boy, serves the food cold. Jason is a bit crabby with him but won't talk about it.

Jason: I don't want to talk about it.

Medea: That boy doesn't like me. I can tell.

Maid: If I were you I'd ask myself what is wrong with this picture.

Medea: What is wrong with this picture?

Jason: What?

Medea: What about you and the cabin boy, that's what.

Jason: It's nothing. And I don't want to talk about it.

Medea: Well, I think he is pining with love for you. And he hates me because he's jealous. That's what I think.

Jason: He's just a cabin boy. You don't know anything about it. I've got to go now. I've got knots to tie and sails to set.

Medea: I see. Well, I didn't get anywhere with that one.

Maid: This won't last. They're an oil and water mixture.

Medea: Brew me another potion to help me sleep, preferably till we reach land.

Cleo: So she does. But Medea doesn't dream of her mother again and she doesn't dream of the princess.

CLEO GATHERS UP HER CARDS. SINGERS START THE "LULLABY."

Singers:
Sleep and swim and dream
my baby
sleep and swim my baby
girl in the land of
dreams, where giants live
in the dreams of giants,
women swim like giants in
the land of dreams.
Sleep and swim and dream
my baby girl.

Cleo: Eventually, they land at Corinth.

THE ARGOS LANDS AT CORINTH.

ACT 1 · SCENE 2

THE CITY OF CORINTH IS IN VIEW.

Cleo: So this is the city of Corinth . . .

All Others: So this is the city of Corinth.

Cleo: Corinth is a large city, full of people scurrying to and fro . . . to and fro . . . Corinth.

All Others: Corinth!

Cleo: When the Argos gets to port, Jason and Medea find that it is not easy to find a place to live. Medea has always lived in a palace or a temple and Jason has never settled anywhere. They aren't sure how it is you actually look for a place to live. So, they send off the maid to look for a home for them.

THE MAID LEAVES THE BOAT AND SEARCHES THE TOWN.

Cleo: It's not easy for her either. Lots of people have to live in the streets. The maid searches and searches . . .

She searches and searches.

Now some things about Corinth.

Chorus/Sonia: (FINDS THE MESSAGE.) Naturally, Corinth has a king, same as Colchis. His name is Crayon and he is a friendlier kind of guy than Medea's father. When he hears about the foreign ship in port, he sends an invitation to Jason to come on up to the palace.

THE MESSENGER GOES TO THE BOAT.

Messenger: Jason, come on up to the palace. Meet the king.

Jason: This is great. I'm going to meet the king. What should I wear?

Medea: What you've got on is fine.

Jason: Maybe this.

CRAYON. "Welcome to my world."

JASON PUTS ON THE GOLDEN FLEECE AND FOLLOWS THE MESSENGER TO THE PALACE.

Medea: He is easily impressed. Come to think of it, why wasn't I invited?

Chorus/Brenda: You're the wife.

Medea: Who asked you?

Chorus/Brenda: Excuse me.

Cleo: Medea is not invited . . .

Chorus/Sonia: Well, she is the wife . . .

Cleo: Jason goes to the palace . . .

Crayon: Crayon's the name, king is the game. I like to keep a positive outlook. Early to bed, early to rise. No hanky panky, just an average kind of guy. Come on hero, big-buddy-hero-dick, welcome to my world! And speaking of my world, let's have a little peek! Where's my world? (THE GLOBE DESCENDS.) Here it is—now, isn't that something? Well speak up, hero-big-dick. What have you got to say for yourself? Cat got your tongue?

Cleo: So Jason tells the king his old war stories and Crayon has a few stories of his own.

Crayon: I got a few stories of my own.

Jason: You tell me your stories. I'll tell you mine. (ASIDE.) I love this guy. (JASON TAKES OFF THE FLEECE AND GIVES IT TO THE KING.) I want you to have this. I mean it.

Crayon: What a guy. A guy that'd give you the fleece off his back. Big hero-dick.

Jason: Big-buddy-king-guy.

Cleo: So, pretty soon they are good buddies, and get into some serious partying. Jason does not come back to the ship for several days.

In the meantime, Medea is stuck in this stuffy cabin.

Medea: I hate this place.

Cleo: . . . and the maid is off house-hunting.

Medea: I'm so mad I could eat sails. I'll get out of here if I have to chew my way out!

Cleo: One day, when the cabin boy comes with her meal, cold as usual, she bonks him on the head. She goes up to the deck. No one sees her leave the ship.

Later, the cabin boy will say she bewitched him by growing larger than normal size and hypnotizing him with a supernatural stare. How else could she, a mere woman, have managed to escape?

By the time she has reached the town, there is a crowd of curious onlookers who want to see the Greek hero's barbarian witch. As I mentioned before, all we know for sure is that she has a green thumb.

They crane their necks to look at her, but no-one speaks to her. Their languages are different. She wanders in the market for a while, hoping she will find the maid . . .

MEDEA FINDS THE MAID.

Medea: I would like something to eat.

Maid: So would I but I have no money and no one knows us here.

Medea: Any luck finding a place?

Maid: Not yet.

Medea: Maybe we should go to the palace.

Maid: Why?

Medea: Well, Jason is there. Maybe the king likes him. Maybe not. Maybe he would help us. Maybe not. I should be there just to see how things work in this place.

Maid: Can't Jason figure it out?

Medea: I'm not sure.

Maid: Where is the palace?

Medea: I don't know.

Maid: And no one will tell us—they don't speak our language.

Medea: I can't think what to do next. This is supposed to be an adventure and it's just a big mess. And now I have to think about this baby.

Maid: I knew it! I knew this would come to no good. A baby! Now you're in it!

Medea: It's supposed to be a happy occasion.

Maid: Happy!

Chorus/Zelda: Well, and god knows where he's off to. Or what he's up to.

Cleo: Well, what can you expect. Hardly away from home and already pregnant. It's enough to make you spit. But that's how it often goes.

Chorus/Zelda: When it happened to me I was at my wit's end. I didn't know what to do. When it happened to my own girl, I didn't know whether to laugh or cry. This is the place where women get trapped.

Chorus/Sonia: Not me.

Chorus/Zelda: That's what you say now. It could happen to anyone.

MEDEA AND THE MAID WANDER THE STREETS. THEY STOP AT THE WOMEN'S TEMPLE. MEDEA AND THE MAID GO INSIDE.

Cleo: Finally, tired and footsore, Medea and the maid stumble upon the women's temple, which is shabbier than it should be and run down, but at least it is still standing. The women there feed them and offer a bath and sit with them, and, after a while, they talk with a few words and gestures.

Temple Woman: Sit down . . . down . . .

Medea: Down . . .

Temple Woman: Rest . . . rest . . .

Maid: Rest . . . she wants us to rest.

Medea: Rest . . .

Temple Woman: Eat . . . eat . . . good.

Maid: Eat . . .

Temple Woman: Sit down . . . down

Medea: Sit . . .

Temple Woman: Name . . .

Medea: Excuse me?

Temple Woman: Name.

Maid: Temple woman . . . name.

Medea: Medea.

Temple Woman: Medea . . . good.

Medea: Name?

Temple Woman: Temple woman . . .

Medea: Oh . . .

Temple Woman: Where from?

Medea: Colchis.

Temple Woman: Why come?

Medea: Husband . . .

Temple Woman: Oh.

Medea: Why did I come here? I hate everything and everyone. I can't find a place to live. I don't know where Jason is . . . and I'm pregnant. Pregnant.

Temple Woman: Baby . . .

Medea: Baby . . . and I'm so miserable. And I want my mother.

Temple Woman: We're sorry. Your mother is not here. Only us. Rest now. Sleep.

Maid: I'll stay with her. I'm used to her.

Cleo: So they stay in the temple for a while to figure things out. They both have to work there and the food is not great but it is a restful place and they will be safe there.

Meanwhile, back at the palace, the party's over. Jason leaves the palace with a hangover and returns to the ship.

Jason: Where's Medea?

Sailor: I don't know and I don't care. I guess you could try the women's temple.

Jason: The women's temple? Why would she go there?

Sailor: That's where they all go when things get tough.

Jason: That place should be banned.

Sailor: You're better off without her.

Jason: Maybe she's pregnant.

Sailor: Oh.

Jason: I better go find her.

Sailor: Whatever . . .

Cleo: So Jason goes to find Medea. He hangs around outside the temple until she comes to talk to him.

Medea: I'm pregnant.

Jason: I knew it.

Medea: I need a home for the baby. I won't go back to the ship. That is that. (MEDEA GOES BACK INTO THE TEMPLE.)

Jason: The honeymoon is over. Of course that is what married life is all about, I guess. How about that? A baby. Now what do I do? The king will know. Maybe he can help me.

Cleo: So, Jason goes back to the palace, where Crayon is talking to his daughter, the princess.

Crayon: How's my princess today?

Princess: Your what?

Crayon: My princess. The darling of my heart, my baby girl.

Princess: Sooner or later, you'll have to let me grow up.

Crayon: Don't be so damned sour. Have a little fun. It won't kill ya. What you need is a husband.

Princess: I am not going to get married.

Crayon: You'll feel different when the time comes.

Princess: I don't think so.

Crayon: Someday your prince will come. When the time is right.

Princess: I think I prefer my horse.

JASON ENTERS.

Crayon: Yo, Jason. How's the boy?

Jason: Gee, big-buddy-king-guy. I don't know what to say.

Crayon: You big dick. I love ya!

Jason: Some big dick, my wife is mad at me. She's gotten herself pregnant. And now I don't know how to please her. I'm doing the best I can but she doesn't see it that way.

Crayon: A family man, eh? Now isn't that something. You know what my daddy always used to say? He used to say, "Son"—he called me Son—"the family is the backbone of the nation." Father-mother-babies, that's what it's all about. A strong nation needs strong families. And a strong family needs a strong father. And strong fathers have strong sons. No problem in that department where you're concerned.

Jason: Yeah, I guess. But what does she want?

Crayon: You tell me.

Jason: It's all just a big headache. I kind of like the idea of the baby. It'd be new . . . it'd be mine . . . but now she wants things . . . I don't get it.

Crayon: Nesting, that's what they do, boy. Best to go along with them. They're not the same as us. They're a different animal altogether. Best just play along with her.

Jason: Thanks, big-buddy-king-guy.

Crayon: So what'll it take, big guy?

Jason: Take?

Crayon: To get her off your back.

Jason: A house, she says. A house.

Crayon: I can get you one of those.

Jason: You can?

Crayon: Sure I can.

Jason: I don't know what to say, big guy.

Crayon: You don't have to say a thing.

Jason: Thanks, big guy.

Crayon: What are friends for, anyway?

Jason: Anything I can do, big guy, just name it.

Crayon: Well, now that you mention it, let's have a look at the world. The big picture. The little picture. You know what I mean. I could use a man like you around here. And here. And here. You know, the world is like an oyster, my boy, and it could be ours. See, people like you, I like you. You are considered a pretty big hero-dick around here because of what you did in the war.

Jason: It was nothing.

Crayon: People are impressed. They're asking if you are planning to stay for a while. How about it?

Jason: Well . . .

Crayon: Corinth isn't a bad place, you know.

Jason: No . . . it's a great place . . .

Crayon: Confidentially, I could use a man like you . . . fight off pirates . . . maybe consolidate a few territorial disputes . . . nothing I can't handle myself, you understand, but hey, there's a job to do and a man for the job. I say let's go . . . what do you say?

Jason: I don't quite follow you, big guy.

Crayon: You got a family coming . . .

Jason: Yeah . . .

Crayon: You scratch my back. I scratch yours.

Jason: Right.

Crayon: Help me take care of business. Make Corinth a safer place for your family.

Jason: Right.

Crayon: Fight fight fight, right?

Jason: Right.

Jason & Crayon: One, two, three, four. Let's have a thumb war. Hug, kiss, get back, fight.

Crayon: Deal?

Jason: Deal.

Princess: Congratulations, Dad.

Crayon: I'm doing it all for you, kid. Just doing my job. (ASIDE.) That kid loves her old dad.

Cleo: A few days later, Jason stands outside the women's temple again. Medea and the maid come out and he leads them to the house that Crayon has given him.

Chorus/Sonia: Look at him. Leading her down the garden path. Does she have any idea what he's doing? Does he?

Cleo: Jason thinks . . .

Jason: I'm a man with a job to do . . . a man with responsibilities.

Cleo: Jason leads Medea to the house that the king has given them. It is outside the city. On a hill. It is small. And no-one has lived in it for some time. It is dirty and the door is off the hinge, but the maid is pleased to learn that she will have her own room.

Maid: I will have my own room.

Cleo: It is late in the day. They eat and go to sleep. The princess pets her horse.

ACT 2

MOTHER LEADS THE ACTORS TO THE STAGE. ACTORS AND SINGERS BEGIN THE "MAIDS" ROUND.

Singers: Always wash the spoons this way
Pile the sheets and towels just so
Stir the porridge counterclockwise
Wax the floor before you go
Make our coffee first this morning
Feed the dog, also the cat
Wash the clothes and clean the cupboards
Dust the tables, bathe the brat . . .

Cleo: There are two kinds of domestic help: live-in and live-out. I have been both. It's hard to say which is better. If you live in you save money—though you will never be paid enough to do this kind of work. If you live out, they don't have so much control over what you do. I found that when I lived in, the people I worked for often felt they could to tell me what to do with my spare time, as if I couldn't figure it out for myself. They would check on what books I was reading. They would set a time when I had to be home at night. I did not have a key to the house. Meals were a big ordeal. There was always a question of where you would eat. If the family eats in the dining room, you eat in the kitchen. But at breakfast, they often eat in the kitchen: do you eat with them? Or wait and eat later? Every family has a different rule. They likely only feed you once a day. The mother and father are working out and you eat with the children. If you live in, you may also share a room with one of the children. Depends. So having your own room is a big deal.

Maid: First thing in the morning. The hillside is quiet, the sun is rising. There are some birds. What a mess this place is. But it can be fixed up, I guess. There is room for a garden.

JASON AND MEDEA WAKE UP AND COME OUT TO LOOK AROUND.

Cleo: Jason and Medea wake up.

THEY ALL SET TO WORK FIXING UP THE PLACE.

Medea: I'm glad that Jason is helping.

Maid: I hope this means that he is taking an interest in his about-to-be family.

Medea: He's doing his best. We should give him the benefit of the doubt.

Maid: Of course. But don't forget to cover your ass.

Medea: You're beginning to sound like my mother.

Maid: Well, she would know.

Jason: This is really boring.

Maid: What did I tell you?

Medea: Stop it! I cannot live like this with you picking everything apart. It doesn't help. We have to at least behave as if things might turn out right! Jason loves me. He's not very good at some things but he does love me. He does try. I'm sure he wants to change. And I will help him.

Maid: What makes you think he wants to change?

Medea: You don't understand the kind of life he's had.

Maid: That doesn't answer my question. Things pretty much go the way he wants them to. He doesn't have any reason to change his ways.

Medea: I couldn't have stayed at home. You must see that. I have to try and make this work. You must see that too.

Maid: I do. And I don't.

Jason: What's all this squabbling?

Maid & Medea: Nothing.

Jason: All I ask is a little peace and quiet.

Cleo: Just in time, the king's messenger turns up.

Messenger: Message for Jason big-hero-dick.

Jason: Yo, messenger.

Messenger: "Jason, my boy, the time has come for us to secure our borders and settle once and for all territorial disputes that threaten the security of the city of Corinth and surrounding lands. It's the least we can do for our friends and allies who rely on us" . . . blah-de-blah-blah. Do you want me to read the rest?

Jason: I get the picture. The big picture. It's what the big guy wants me to do.

Medea: Where are you going?

Jason: I've got a job to do.

Medea: What kind of a job?

Jason: For the king. Top secret. I feel I owe him one. After all, he gave us all this. Really I'm doing it for you. Yeah. I think that's right. It's my job. You know how it is. What would happen if everybody stopped doing their job? Keep the home fires burning and the bun in the oven on warm.

Maid: Look at him go.

Medea: I hate you. You're so smug! He does have a job to do.

Maid: Help me put the door back on its hinge.

Cleo: So here is Jason securing borders. And here is Medea and her maid starting the garden. When Jason comes home, he has money and gifts . . .

Jason: All I want is for you to be happy.

Medea: Is that all?

Jason: I mean that. I really do.

Cleo: Then he goes to drink with his sailor buddies and Crayon.

Medea: The baby will change things. I know that. I am more and more full of dreams of it coming.

SINGERS BEGIN THE "NEW BABY" ROUND.

Singers: Every baby girl who comes is a new
idea arriving looking for her place
Every new idea arrives like a baby
girl looking for her mother
Every new mother arrives looking for
her baby girl . . .

THE BABY GIRL ARRIVES, BROUGHT TO MEDEA BY MOTHER.

Mother: . . . or that is how it should be . . .

. . . I am so sorry, my Medea, that I wished you were a boy. You were a wonderful baby, full of life, and I should have wanted you more than I did and later I was not able to show you how to be stronger than I am myself. I am sorry now for all the misery of your past, for your father's treachery, and your brother's creepiness, but now, when you have the chance, make your baby stronger than I was and stronger than yourself so that she is not lost in her dreams wondering what to do with her life . . .

Medea: (MEDEA CUDDLES HER BABY.) Your life will be different from my own.

Maid: You know what my grandmother used to say? "She will learn what she sees you do."

Cleo: This is how their lives go . . . Jason sails off to fight pirates and comes home and fights with Medea and drinks with his friends and they make up and make love and pretty soon there is another baby. The children plague their mother and are spoiled by their father and the maid likes them but finds them tiresome at times.

Maid: These kids are awful brats.

MEDEA WALKS DOWN THE HILL TO THE TEMPLE.

Cleo: Once a month, Medea leaves the children with the maid and goes to the women's temple for a few days. This is considered old-fashioned of her. The local people think that the women's temple is kind of funny. The men prefer their own gods and keep the women away from the old temple where, they say, the women are just encouraged to cling to old habits and really they are better off at home. The women in the temple talk among themselves that maybe the men are so discouraging because they hate women to be together for any reason, but gradually they can see that the new fashion in gods is taking hold and women feel tied to men through their children.

MEDEA ENTERS THE TEMPLE.

Cleo: I love my children.

Medea: I love my children.

Chorus/Zelda: And Jason is not so bad . . .

Medea: And Jason is not so bad . . .

Chorus/Brenda: Things could be worse.

Medea: Things could be worse, but I need people to talk to . . . I need to figure out what I'll do with the rest of my life.

Temple Woman & Medea: CHANTING WITH SINGERS.

Talk to me
Brush my hair

Sit with me
Tell me stories
Tell me what your life is
like
And I will tell you mine
Tell me all your children's
names
Can a woman live alone
Can she make a life of her
own
With no man unless she
pleases
Talk to me
Help me figure this out . . .

NIGHT FALLS.

Cleo: In the house, the maid puts the children to bed.

Maid: I miss the temple. I used to go there for a day now and then, but now that there are children, I hardly get to leave the house.

THE MAID DRINKS A CUP OF TEA.

Cleo: Meanwhile, at the palace . . .

Princess: Life goes on in its back-stabbing hissy fit way . . .

Crayon: Hello Princess.

Princess: I wish you'd stop calling me that.

Crayon: It's your name. It's time you did a little growing up. You were born Princess and that's who you are. You're lucky. Not every girl gets to be a princess. A lot of girls would like to be in your shoes. You can't get away from it by changing your name.

Princess: I hate this place.

Crayon: That's natural. You're a stubborn one. Just like your mother.

Princess: My mother hardly ever leaves her room.

Crayon: She always gets what she wants, though. You know, I got a lot of respect for women. They're tricky. You don't want to mess with them. You don't have to worry about your old mum.

Princess: I'm not.

Crayon: Of course a lot of men like women to be soft, but me, I don't like the dumb bunny type. Never did. Of course your really smart woman knows better than to show it.

Princess: What are you getting at, Dad?

Crayon: I may be the king but I got my troubles too. You might want to think about that. If things go badly for me here they're not going to go good for you.

Princess: What does that mean?

Crayon: I got enemies, you know. Not everybody is working in the best interest of the nation.

Princess: What is the best interest of the nation?

Crayon: That's my girl. I love it when you take an interest. See, I got the big guy Jason hero-dick out there settling the territorial disputes but I got trouble at home too. Some people in the court are saying Corinth is a dump. Behind the times. They want to boost trade with the outlying territories. And they're right.

Princess: So?

Crayon: Well, I have to spend money fixing the place up. Spend money to make money, get it? Tear down the old market-place. Maybe the women's temple . . .

Princess: Oh . . .

Crayon: Maybe we wouldn't have to . . . the old place is a bit of an eyesore, though. Lots of people have brought it up . . . they say we should move with the times . . .

Princess: Get rid of the women's temple . . .

Crayon: Just an idea, of course. But don't you worry your pretty little head. Your old dad will look after it. You can always rely on your old dad, Princess. You know that.

Princess: Why are you telling me this?

Crayon: Well, I think you're right. It is time I let you grow up. No more little princess. You're a woman now. Time to be thinking about that husband. We need some new blood in the family. I can't go on forever. But don't you worry about it. Nice horse you got there. When did I give that to you? Last birthday? Nothing is too good for my princess.

Princess: I think I see what you're up to.

Crayon: I'm doing it all for you . . . Princess.

JASON ENTERS. THE PRINCESS LISTENS TO THEM.

Jason: Yo, king-guy.

Crayon: Jason big-dick.

Jason: Big-buddy-king-guy.

Crayon: Jason, the son that I have always wanted.

Jason: (ASIDE.) I like it when the big guy talks this way.

Crayon: Jason, my son. You know, you should be my son. And, come to think of it, you could be.

Jason: I don't follow you, big guy.

Crayon: You could marry my daughter.

Cleo: Privately, Crayon is thinking . . .

Crayon: (ASIDE.) I have enemies at home as well as in the disputed territories. This boy is as thick as two planks, but nobody messes with him. And he has a grateful nature. A man like him in the family would consolidate matters. Take care of the Princess too. I don't like the way she talks about that horse. (TO

JASON.) What do you say to that, Jason? Your children would inherit all this.

Chorus/Annie: Marry the boss's daughter?

Cleo: That's what it looks like.

Chorus/Annie: I don't believe it.

Cleo: Believe it. It happens all the time.

Chorus/Annie: You don't have to look so smug.

Cleo: I'm not. But I can't see him stepping out of line.

Jason: I'm married already. I have two kids.

Cleo: Jason is thinking . . .

Jason: (ASIDE.) This is incredible. What an opportunity. The thing about Medea is she doesn't quite get how things work. She doesn't realize how hard it is for me out there. This princess would be different because her father is the king and she'd probably know what it takes. I have had a look at her, too. She is young. She has never spoken to me and I have never heard her laugh, which makes me think that she might be soft and quiet and gentle, as I believe women should be. (TO CRAYON.) Yo, big guy, what can I say? What can I do?

Crayon: Nothing, my boy, nothing. I can take care of it all. See I've been thinking . . . the thing is people are suspicious of foreigners in these parts.

Jason: Suspicious?

Crayon: Of course everybody loves a sailor, so big hero-dicks like you are different, but well, you know how people are and so I was thinking I could make a law that foreigners couldn't live here.

Jason: Oh.

Crayon: Or, if push comes to shove, we could just kill her. Whatever it takes.

Jason: Whatever it takes.

Crayon: That's right, boy, hard ball.

Jason: Hard ball.

Crayon: You got it.

Jason: Hey, big guy, I'm with you all the way, but look, we wouldn't have to kill her would we? You know she gets lonely and I think she misses home. I could just send her back—she has family there—and let her take the kids. They are too young to be away from their mother. We don't have to kill her, I don't think.

Crayon: Whatever you say, big-dick. I can't say no to ya. I love ya that much.

Jason: I mean, she is a bit of a bitch sometimes but she's not bad as women go . . . it's just that . . . hey, big guy . . . am I doing okay?

Crayon: You're doing fine. Leave it all to me.

Cleo: So the deal is made. Now, what about the king's daughter? Here she is, in the courtyard of the king's house.

THE KING GOES TO HIS DAUGHTER.

Princess: Forget it. I won't do it. For one thing, he is already married.

Crayon: I'll deal with that. I'll change the law or whatever it takes.

Princess: I said forget it.

Crayon: It's in your own best interest to go along with this.

Princess: I see what this means for me. I must marry this guy and start making babies to consolidate your position.

Crayon: You don't have to look at it like that.

Princess: I don't want to marry him.

Crayon: You'll get over it.

Princess: I don't want to marry anyone. I hate the whole business.

Crayon: That's how you see it now. But you'll see that this is how it's going to be. You'll change your mind.

Princess: In a pig's eye.

Cleo: She gets up and goes to feed her horse. Her mother waves from the window. (THE QUEEN WAVES.) Her mother will be no help to her. She only wants to stay out of the way as much as possible. The king hates his wife because she did not make sons. Mother is pleased about this marriage. Maybe now Crayon will calm down. She just wishes her daughter would show a little more interest.

Queen: I just wish she'd show a little interest.

JASON HIDES BEHIND THE HORSE.
HE JUMPS OUT WHEN THE PRINCESS
COMES TO FEED IT.

Jason: Boo!

Princess: Jerk!

Crayon: That girl's got spirit! She's always been a handful! I kind of like it.

Jason: Gee, big guy. Are you sure she likes me?

Crayon: Sure she does. They're all shy to begin with. She's just got to get used to the idea. A firm hand. That's what she needs.

Jason: Whatever, big guy.

Cleo: Actually, the king has only tried to beat his daughter once. She bit him on the knee, drawing blood. He still has the tooth marks.

So, what will all this bunch of people do? Jason is cleaning his weapons. Medea is digging in the garden, and the maid is doing laundry. The kids are having a nap. Crayon is dodging his enemies at court. And the queen is probably dodging Crayon. Their daughter is sulking in her room.

Cleo & Others: Another day in Corinth.

Cleo: And now, the king's messenger is trudging up the hill, but it is so hot that he stops to rest for a while. Medea and the maid stop working. They lie down under a tree to get out of the sun.

Personally, I never got to be what I'd call the friend of any of the people I worked for. Friendship with your employer is a loaded gun, and the employer is holding it. Like most maids, servants, and domestic help, I kept my distance. They are your friends now, this minute, because they are lonely, like Medea, or because their own friends have deserted them, or their lovers have walked out, or the men on whom they depend have done them wrong . . . but when they have sorted out their troubles in some way it is you who must scrub their floor. And they will be embarrassed that they told you their secrets. And their talk about how all us women have a common experience, no matter what colour our skin is or how well off we are, all that is forgotten. So, even though the maid has been given this time to rest under the same tree as Medea, she sleeps light, because you never know. Medea, lonely for her husband, tired out by work and the summer heat, sleeps like the dead.

The king's messenger arrives at the gate. The maid wakes up.

THE MAID GOES TO THE GATE.

Messenger: Where is Medea?

Maid: Sleeping.

Messenger: Wake her up.

Maid: Can't it wait?

Messenger: It's from the king.

Maid: All right, all right. Don't get your shirt in a knot.

Medea: What's going on?

Maid: The king's messenger is at the gate.

Medea: Where are the children?

Maid: Asleep.

Cleo: Medea, followed by her maid, goes to the gate to meet the messenger. The messenger hands Medea a letter.

Medea: I can't read this language.

Messenger: No problem. "You are banished from the city of Corinth and from the land around it. Leave before dawn." Signed, Crayon, the king.

Medea: That's it? That's all? Just leave?

Messenger: I'm only the messenger.

Medea: Get out.

Cleo: The messenger leaves.

Medea: Where are the children?

Maid: Asleep.

Medea: I want you to wake them up. Take them to the women's temple. Ask the women to look after them until I send for them. Go by the back streets so no one from the palace sees you. Do it now.

Maid: What will you do?

Medea: What do you think? I will leave. It's not safe for me here. I can't go home. And I must find a place for myself in the world . . . and for the children . . .

Maid: How will you manage on your own like that? You should let me come with you.

Medea: You?

Maid: Me and the children. We should stick together.

Medea: We can't. It's not safe. The children will be fine in the temple. You will have to do the best you can. Later you may be able to come to me with the children.

Maid: I have looked after you since your mother died. I looked after your mother, too. Your mother was killed by your father, and Jason . . .

Medea: We don't know what Jason has to do with this.

Maid: Don't make excuses for him.

Medea: I'm not. I'm just saying we don't know. He's not strong. He would go along with the king's plans. Maybe without realizing what it meant. I don't know.

Maid: No, you don't.

Medea: If I could talk to him . . .

Maid: There's no time. And talk is cheap. What matters is what we do—now.

Medea: We need time to figure that out. And time is what we never have. There's no planning—everything just happens.

Maid: We stand a better chance if we stick together.

Medea: Too risky . . . take the children . . . please . . . take them to the temple . . . go now.

Cleo: The maid took the children and went as she was told, leaving Medea alone. At this time, Medea feels herself larger than normal size and she screams . . .

Medea: Mother!!!!!!!!

MOTHER ENTERS.

Medea: How could this happen?

Mother: What has happened exactly?

Medea: The king has thrown me out of Corinth and I don't know where my husband is.

Mother: You never knew that, but why did the king throw you out?

Medea: I don't know. He must have some plan for Jason.

Mother: I'm not surprised. He probably has someone else he wants Jason to marry. Maybe his daughter.

Medea: Marry the boss's daughter? I don't believe it. She's hardly more than a child.

Mother: They like them young.

Medea: Mother, that's awful.

Mother: It's an old story.

Medea: Now what do I do?

Mother: You've already decided that, I think. You're going to leave town.

Medea: It was too risky to travel with the maid and the children.

Mother: You will have to find a way to make a living.

Medea: How will I do that? It's very frightening. Who will help me?

Mother: When push comes to shove, you are what you've got. Smart women know that.

Medea: You are not very comforting. In fact, you never were.

Mother: There's not much comfort in the world when it all boils down. Men and women don't get along most of the time. Men are afraid of women laughing at them and women fear that men will rape or kill them. The rest just follows. What comfort is there in that?

Medea: If that's true, why do we bother to keep going at all?

Mother: I think mating makes people optimistic. At first. But after that the best thing is to be strong and cunning—your own toughness is your comfort. I wish I had done better by you. My daughter . . . my sweet baby . . . you have to be as hard as nails just to get through the day. But now is the time to start. Get out of my dreamland and fend for yourself.

Medea: Is that all you've got to say?

Mother: Why should the dead have any more sense than the living? Do the best you can.

Medea: Is that enough?

Mother: If it isn't, I don't know what is.

MEDEA IS IN HER OWN GARDEN AGAIN. SHE DESTROYS THE HOUSE AND LEAVES.

Cleo: It breaks my heart to think of her going through all this. It seems the only way to learn is through experience. But then it's too late.

Of course, Medea never saw Jason again.

Cleo & Others: When the king sends the messenger back to the house next day, no one is there, but every dish in the house is broken, and the garden uprooted and the animals loose in the yard.

Cleo: The queen goes to her daughter's room to dress her for the wedding, but the princess has covered herself with desiccated field rats, which is pretty scary.

Crayon: She's a great disappointment to her old dad. I was too easy on her. I see that now. Spare the rod and spoil the child. Take her to a dungeon, lock her up, starve her. Whatever. She'll come around. Of course, some of this I blame on her mother, you know. She never took an interest in my work.

Cleo: While Jason meets his buddies in a tavern in the market, while Crayon starts to think about his empire and his dinner, while the queen starts a headache and goes to her room, their daughter falls asleep in the dungeon and dreams . . .

Princess: I dream that I am larger than life and can wrap my legs around the moon. I am swept up by a woman dressed in honey and fire who carries me to a rock where an old woman sits drinking tea. The old woman says,

Mother: I had a daughter. I failed to tell her things before I died and now nothing that I say is much use to her. I came here on the off-chance that I might help you. Maybe you can save yourself from these men and their plans for your life.

My advice to you is tell them nothing. Then strike when they least expect it. That's the law of the land.

Princess: That is sort of what I was planning.

Mother: Good for you.

Princess: Nice chatting with you.

Mother: Thank you.

Cleo: Then she is dumped back on the floor and wakes up.

Jason: Medea left without even saying goodbye. She didn't even give me a chance to explain. But I can't say I blame her. It must be a big disappointment. How is she going to get along on her own? I could have helped her out. She didn't have to run off like that. What's the matter with her? Why can't women just be soft and gentle and nice?

Crayon: There's no figuring them out, my boy. Be firm. Be strong. Don't let them get away with anything.

Jason: I wish I knew where Medea is and where she took the kids.

Cleo: Where is Medea? She's gone. On her own for the first time. That will be hard, but I guess it's not the worst thing that can happen.

After some days, Crayon releases a pale and chastened daughter from the dungeon. She says nothing. Her head is bowed. She is dressed and perfumed for the wedding.

Jason finds himself cheering up a bit. Life must go on.

The ceremony is long and elaborate. The bride says nothing but that which is required.

Jason is pleased. She is, after all, younger than Medea, and very beautiful, and quiet.

After the marriage, he takes her to bed. He rapes her. She does not struggle. When he falls asleep, she gets up, dresses in dark clothing and sets fire to the marriage bed. She goes to the women's temple. The women help her leave the city.

When Jason awakens, his bed is on fire, and his bride is gone.

Crayon: This whole thing has gone far enough. It's the women who've messed this up. They have to be brought in line. Show them who's boss. Who's the Big Dick around here anyway? One thing to consider is the women's temple. And the whole marketplace area. That temple is an eyesore and it's in the way. If they can't look after it they can't have it. I get all kinds of complaints and I'm fed up. We've got to clean things up around here.

Cleo: That night, a gang of thugs storm the temple, destroy the place and kill many of the women.

Crayon: Nobody knows how it happened. A terrible tragedy. But like I say, the place was an eyesore. Trouble was bound to happen. You could see it a mile away.

Cleo: You could, too.

Crayon: Naturally there will be a complete investigation.

Cleo: The court decides that the women's carelessness

about the condition of the temple property incited the men to violence and has ordered them to restore the temple to its original condition within the day. This is not possible, of course.

Crayon: Maybe next time they'll know.

Cleo: Know what? That's the question.

Chorus/Zelda: If a man gets riled up there's no telling what he'll do. The women's temple is destroyed and warrants are issued for the arrest of those suspected of being temple women. The women scatter, hide, move on. The temple is now a crumbling ruin. I think they should have kept the place tidier. Looked after it more. And not been so obvious about themselves. That way they wouldn't have drawn attention to themselves.

Cleo: What is the upshot of all this? The king died eventually, when a knife wound turned septic.

Chorus/Brenda: The queen was pensioned off to a small farm.

Jason: After the fire, I left the women alone unless one got in my way.

Chorus/Brenda: He died when the prow of his rotting ship fell on him, as he slept through a hangover.

Jason: A great hero in my prime—a tragic accident at the end.

Princess: I escaped and led my life assisted by the ghost of Medea's mother. If I'm gonna be a target, I'm gonna be a moving one.

Cleo: And Medea? Stories were circulated about her wickedness and enchantments. They say she killed the king's daughter with poison and murdered her own children.

Medea: They can say what they like. I am living to be an old woman. Older than my mother. And without my children. They never had a chance. I heard about the temple and what happened there. I will mourn till I die.

Maid: I think Medea was a woman more or less like any other who depended on a man and got no thanks for it. I wish she had listened to me. I wish I knew where she was and what happened to her. Of course, I didn't do what she told me. I took the children and left the country. They have lived with me since then. Worse things could have happened, I suppose, but she must be lonely without her children. When I heard about the women's temple, I thought my heart would break.

SINGERS START THE "MOTHER" ROUND. CHORUS JOINS.

Singers:
One step, another step, another step, another step,
Now you are walking,
One word, another word, another word, another word,
Now you are talking,
Never stop moving, Never shut your mouth
One thought, another thought, another thought, another thought,
Now you are thinking,
Never stop thinking,
Mothers and daughters
Never stop moving,
Never shut your mouths full of honey and words
Never stop . . .

Mother: Mothers, make your daughters strong. That's all I've got to say.

Cleo: And the maid . . . had to find another job.

So there you have it. The big story. I don't think it's such a big deal in itself. It's a big deal because it happens every day. My neighbour in the Supersave says it shows how the other half lives. The other half of what? I say.

JACKIE CROSSLAND has been working in Canadian alternative theatre for many years as an actor, playwright and director. Her plays have been performed in Vancouver, Toronto, Montreal and Los Angeles. In recent years, Ms. Crossland has been working with Nora D. Randall in their storytelling company, Random Acts. They tell stories about the lives of working women and lesbians, appearing before union meetings, conferences, and community organizations, and in arts festivals. *Collateral Damage: The Tragedy of Medea* is in many ways directly linked to the storytelling experience Ms. Crossland has gained within this company. "Telling stories is a familiar thing, like coming home. It is an empowering act bacause the listener has as many stories as the teller and they can easily trade places."

Press Gang Publishers Feminist Co-operative is committed to publishing a wide range of writing by women which explores themes of personal and political struggles for equality.

A free listing of our books is available from Press Gang Publishers, 603 Powell Street, Vancouver, B.C. V6A 1H2 Canada

Printed in Canada